GIRL

By Gerald Green

Fiction

Nonfiction

GIRL

by Gerald Green

DOUBLEDAY & COMPANY, INC.
GARDEN CITY, NEW YORK
1977

Library of Congress Cataloging in Publication Data
Green, Gerald.
   Girl.
    1. Dogs—Legends and stories. I. Title.
PZ3.G8227Gi   [PS3513.R4493]   813'.5'4
ISBN 0-385-11650-0
Library of Congress Catalog Card Number 76-12051

GIRL

Groff, the producer, smelled the visitors before he saw them. He looked up from his IBM Selectric, on which he was writing questions for an interview with a senator, and saw an old man and a dog. The musty odor was laminated, multileveled. The man smelled of barns, compost heaps, rural debris. The dog smelled like an old dog.

"Yes?" Groff asked.

"This here is the Don Derry show."

"Do you have an appointment?" Groff, a Phi Beta Kappa from New York University, a starved, trembling man, was always polite to the oddballs, losers, and misfits who managed to sneak into the office. There but for the grace of network television went Alan Groff.

"The lady outside said it was okay."

Groff picked up the phone and bawled out the receptionist.

"I couldn't help it, Alan," the girl said. "You've never seen an act like he has. Don will love it. That *dog!*"

Groff sighed. Everyone was a producer. Everyone auditioned acts. He prided himself on knowing Don Derry's mercurial tastes, anticipating the star's notions of programing. At the moment Derry was in a "serious" phase. Breast cancer, impotence, ecology. Groff was fairly certain Derry was not interested in a white-bearded bum and a scruffy mutt. But he was a tolerant man.

"Okay. What do you do? Mr. . . . ?"

"Mr. Riddle. This dog is named Girl."

"I'm waiting."

"This dog, Girl, has a vocabulary of more

than four thousand words. Taught her myself. This dog understands the English language."

Liz Willis, the script girl, got up from a rear desk and walked toward the front of the office. The writers and secretaries stayed with their scripts and phone calls. An old man, looking like a disreputable Santa, and a grayish-brown mongrel were not subjects for special interest. Two days ago a man had escorted in an enormous squawking ostrich which had defecated on the director's desk.

"Convince me," Groff said.

"Certainly. Girl, listen to me."

The dog, slouched against Mr. Riddle's leg, struggled to a standing position. She was about the size of an airedale and was covered with tight curls. In conformation, the dog appeared to be a combination of old English sheepdog and possibly one of the larger terriers. The muzzle and the hairs around the eyes were white. She had floppy white paws. When

Girl yawned, the soft jowls trembled, as if the effort were too much for her old head.

"We're waiting," Liz Willis said politely.

"Girl, show me the pretty blond lady in the green dress."

The dog walked over to Liz and placed a paw on her thigh. The script girl patted Girl's head.

"Girl, show us the telephone. The one on this man's desk."

With no hesitation, the dog wheeled away from Liz, and placed forepaws on Groff's phone.

"Show me the machine that sends the news."

"Impossible," Groff said. "She can't know that."

The dog padded across the office, sniffed the air a few times, and as the writers stared, pressed her wet nose against the Associated Press teleprinter.

Groff looked at Liz. "Not bad. It's a trick, of course."

"Conditioning, I suppose. Reinforcing. The way they train pigeons and chickens." Liz smiled at Mr. Riddle. "What else can she do?"

"Ma'am, just about anything, so long as Girl understands."

"Will she obey anyone else?" Groff asked.

"I'm afraid not. You see, E. J. Riddle, that's me, trained her, and it's E. J. Riddle she obeys. Girl, there's two young men in back of the room. Find me the one with the funny yellow sweater that goes all around his neck."

The dog turned from the AP machine. In slow, dignified steps she walked toward the writer who was wearing a yellow turtle-neck sweater.

"Show me where they are making coffee," Mr. Riddle said.

Girl swiveled her head. The eyes, Groff noted, were luminous and bright. Lights winked in the liquid brown. Groff saw intelligence, mysterious beauty in the gentle eyes.

"I said the *coffee*, Girl."

The dog walked toward Liz Willis' filing cabinet, on top of which stood an electric coffee maker. Unable to reach the top of the case, Girl whimpered and pointed her snout upward, as if apologizing.

"Clever, very clever," Groff said. "Even if it's a trick."

"It's no trick," Mr. Riddle said. Girl returned to her master. She sat at Mr. Riddle's feet. Her pink tongue darted in and out of the soft mouth.

"But you must be signaling or directing her," Groff said. Years ago at New York University, he had studied psychology, behaviorism, theories of animal learning.

"No. She understands."

Liz asked: "Are you professional entertainers? Are you an animal trainer?"

"Me and Girl are friends. Had her since she was a pup. We get around. Pass the hat at county fairs. Getting ready to head south, when I seen Mr. Derry a few weeks ago with that rabbit that tap-danced. Heck, I said, Girl is smarter than that."

Groff got up. He looked at Liz. "Don is down on animal acts," he said. "But what the heck? It might be good for some laughs. Maybe after the debate on vasectomy tonight."

Inside his lavish offices, the star of "Don Derry Tonight!" was being measured for a scuba-diving wet suit. The program was going to originate from Nassau in the Bahamas. Derry, a slender, pale man with wheat-colored hair and tiny features concentrated in the middle of a long-jawed head, was in his underwear. A tanned young man from an undersea exploration company was taking his measurements.

7

Groff knocked and peeked in. "Don? Can I bother you with a trained-dog act?"

"It's no act," Mr. Riddle said to Liz. "It's a dog that knows words."

Derry was in a good mood. He had just negotiated a ten-year contract in excess of $500,000 a year. "Yeah, yeah," he said.

Groff held the door open for Mr. Riddle and Girl. Derry's nose recoiled as the old man and the old dog entered.

"This is Mr. Riddle and his dog, Girl," Groff said. "Go ahead Mr. Riddle."

"That there is Mr. Don Derry, Girl. We see him from time to time on the television. How do, sir."

"Hi, Dad."

"Girl, show us Mr. Derry's suit what he took off."

Derry's four-hundred-dollar Cardin suit was draped on a fancy clothes rack in the corner. His two-hundred-dollar crocodile shoes

8

nested beneath the knife-creased trousers and the flared cashmere jacket. Girl placed a furry paw on the pants.

"Show me his shoes, Girl."

The paw moved down to the brown loafers.

"Alan," Don Derry said wearily, "I don't want dogs. The show's growing up, dig?"

"Where's the man in his underwear, Girl?" Mr. Riddle asked.

Girl padded across the orange carpeting and nuzzled Derry's white silk drawers.

"What is this?" Derry laughed. "A gay dog?"

"Don, the dog is fantastic," Liz said. "Mr. Riddle says she understands four thousand words. We could use a few laughs tonight."

"No dog," Derry said. "Besides, he's signaling. He's moving the mutt with signals."

"It ain't signals, Mr. Derry," Mr. Riddle said. "Girl understands me."

"I've seen this number before. Easy stuff —window, chair, clothing, man. He moves the dog. Whistles, something." The TV star held his hands up high while the underwater expert measured his chest.

"Girl, find me the underwater equipment in this room."

Resting against the coffee table was an aqualung, a mask, and flippers. Girl walked over to the gear and put a paw on the yellow oxygen tanks.

"The mask, Girl."

The dog touched the black rubber mask.

"The things for the feet."

The dog put her paw on the black flippers.

"Girl, listen to me. Where is the man going to wear those things?"

Liz raised her eyebrows and looked at Groff. "Oh no, not a magician also. She can't produce Paradise Island on cue."

"Or a hypnotist," Groff said. "She'll make us all *think* we're in a swimming pool."

10

The dog looked puzzled. She moved a step and stared at Mr. Riddle. The shaggy tail wagged furiously. She seemed to want nothing more than to please her master.

"Girl, you *listen* to me," the old man said. "You find me what Mr. Derry uses that equipment in."

The furry head swiveled. The intelligent brown eyes rested on a tank of tropical fish on the window ledge. Girl trotted to the tank and licked the glass.

Everyone except Derry applauded.

"Don, the show's pretty heavy tonight," Liz said. "What can we lose?"

Derry made a gesture of surrender. "Okay, okay. Alan, hang around, please. Liz sweetie, get them cleaned up, huh? Baths, new clothing. That dog has halitosis of the fur."

Mr. Riddle did not seem insulted. He and Girl left with Liz. On the way out, Derry could hear the old man saying: "Girl, I want you to thank this young lady by nodding your head three times."

"Alan," Derry said craftily, "we'll expose the old faker. It has to be a fake. Get me some books on animal psychology. We'll let the guy do his number and then hang them. Dig?"

"A nice old guy like that?"

"But it's phony."

The man from the underwater firm agreed with Derry. "I believe Mr. Derry's right. I've worked with dolphins. It's all done with rewards, food. That dog is nothing special."

Groff, feeling sorry for Mr. Riddle and Girl, sent his secretary out for some books on animal training and the complete works of B. F. Skinner.

For their television appearance, Mr. Riddle and Girl were cleaned up. Liz Willis got a hotel room for the old man, but he used it only to bathe and change into a clean blue flannel shirt. He still wore his red galluses, baggy brown corduroy trousers, and heavy work shoes. He combed Girl and dusted her with deodorant powder but refused to give her a bath. "Girl's an old dog, young lady," he said. "Don't like for her to catch a chill in this damp New York weather."

Mr. Riddle agreed to have his long hair and flowing beard—snowy white and stained with yellow—combed out by a barber. "Feel like a dang trapeze performer," he said. "They are the most fussy kind of people."

Liz worried about where he would stay. Mr. Riddle took her to a rusted green Pierce-Arrow parked under the West Side Highway north of Columbia University. When the taxi approached, Girl began to bark. Her tail wagged violently.

"You live in the car?" Liz asked.

"Oh, it's fine for us."

"But . . . the two of you?"

"Three. There's Alex also."

A savage barking exploded from the Pierce-Arrow. Girl leaped against the rusted doors, whimpering, pawing at the handle.

"Alex?"

"Yep. He's with us. Alex isn't too smart. He's sort of a mastiff. Girl needs a companion as we travel around." His eyes vanished as he chuckled. "Nothing 'tween 'em, young lady. They're both too old. Besides, Girl is an old maid, if you get my drift."

From the rear of the car—the seat had been removed to create a dusty pit—a squashed canine face bared its fangs and barked, then stopped as Mr. Riddle opened the door and let Girl climb in. There were old blankets, bleached dry bones, rubber balls in the murky interior of the car.

"I think we'd better get back to the studio. You and Girl will want to rest up for tonight."

14

"Don't need no rest for doing what we just do as man and dog."

"Can I buy you dinner?"

"A bowl of chili beans will do fine for me."

Liz and Mr. Riddle sat in a small Mexican restaurant below the elevated tracks on Broadway. The old man was true to his word. A bowl of chili and a glass of milk was all he wanted. He ate slowly, neatly. Liz drank coffee and listened to him. He seemed to enjoy talking. She had the impression that his lonely vagabond's life, while of his own choosing, sometimes filled him with the need for human contact and conversation.

"This here chili is tolerably good," Mr. Riddle said. "But the best I ever had was in a small place run by a Chinese gentleman in Flagstaff, Arizona."

"Really?"

"Shows how the world is a surprising place. Full of the unexpected. Imagine a Chinese person cooking the best chili in the world. With big chunks of lean beef and just the right kind of spices. That sauce was so red it was almost black. The world is full of wonder, if you look for it."

"You sound like a poet, Mr. Riddle."

"No, just an old farmer who went broke. Back in nineteen and thirty-six. The land went to dust. Banks foreclosed on me and Mrs. Riddle. She died of the broken heart. That was outside Hastings, Nebraska. I never had the heart to farm none after that."

Liz blinked. He was talking about something that had happened *forty* years ago. "What did you do then?"

"Oh, wandered around. Worked as a hired hand. I always had a way with animals. I could get the most ornery mule to work. Talked a Holstein bull once into getting into a stall when what he really wanted was to kill the farmer who jabbed at him with a pitchfork."

"Animals understood you?"

"Oh, I don't know. I don't make no fancy claims. Some do, some don't. But it never hurts to talk gentle to them. To try to understand the critters. You see, miss, animals and birds and such, they've got as much right to this earth as we do. They're alive. They contribute. Don't matter if it's a plain old dog like Girl, or big Alex, who just keeps me company, or a poor cow, or a chicken, or a wild thing like a fox or a sparrow. They're alive. They got a place set aside for them. They make us laugh, or feel good. I could never abide hunting or that sort of thing."

"But you do talk to animals, don't you?"

"Only when I have the feeling they want talk. It don't matter if they don't understand. I just have the notion someone from our side of the fence, people that is, have an obligation to be civil to them, considering all the harm we've done them." Mr. Riddle chuckled, and closed his crinkled old eyes. "Say, I knew a feller once in Tucson helped a badger dig a hole. Darn badger was running away from some dogs, and that man—he was a naturalist—he got on all fours and dug away with her. You believe that, miss?"

Liz laughed. "If you say so. Tell me. What happened after you worked on farms?"

"I worked all over. There's a bit of a gypsy in E. J. Riddle, I guess. I'm past eighty, but I can't sit still. I mined for the uranium out in Colorado, worked on them big excavations up in Oregon for the dams. Even helped saddle up mules in Grand Canyon. And I always had me a few dogs."

"Any special kind of dogs?"

"Mixed breeds. It got so I couldn't feel comfortable with folks, not since Mrs. Riddle died, and having no children, and being of a shy nature, I took to dogs. Got so I could train them in a few days. You know, roll over, beg, speak, that sort of thing. Trouble was, I'd get so attached to them I couldn't let them go. They interfered with my livelihood."

"When did you get Girl?"

"Now let's see." Mr. Riddle put a gently shaking hand to his forehead. His skin, Liz saw, was like parchment. "Girl is twelve now. Had her a birthday just a month ago when we was at the Shrine Circus down by Tampa. We do our little performance outside the grounds and I pass the hat. Yes, Girl is twelve, and getting smarter every day. I had her since she was a few weeks old."

"But how did you find her?"

"A stray. Like all the dogs I raised. Whining and shivering, around the city dump in Chattanooga. Lovely city, that. They got the big battlefield outside. Can't think of the name, but there was a general they called Pap fought there."

"So you found her alone, as if someone had thrown her out?"

"I reckon. She was a miserable little mutt. What scared me was the place was full of the biggest rats I ever saw. What they couldn't do to a defenseless pup like that! I carried her into my Pierce-Arrow, being the same automobile you saw down below, and I nursed her along. Might I have another glass of milk, miss? Is it all right, you spending Mr. Derry's money like this on me?"

Liz smiled and shook her head. She thought of the two-hundred-dollar lunches, the bloated expense accounts, the gifts of Gucci luggage and Pucci dresses that oiled the business. It depended on one's background and point of view, she decided. Old Riddle was guilty about having a second glass of milk on the program's budget. "Of course," she said. "Some dessert?"

"Oh no. I can't abuse your hospitality, and

I'm more than satisfied with the fine dinner. Anyway, you asked me how Girl learned so much. I saw right away she was no ordinary dog. I always had that talent with animals."

"You began to teach her words? Systematically?"

Mr. Riddle drained his milk. Flecks of white dotted his yellowed mustache, clung to his lips. "You might say. I think more rightly we taught each other. Girl listened and learned, and I got to know her mind. I'd see that bright light in her eyes, and I knew she understood. I tell you what was also involved."

"What, Mr. Riddle?"

"She ain't ever got angry with me or anyone else. Girl is the sweetest-tempered, gentlest animal I have ever observed. Would you believe I have never seen a hair raise on her back, or her lips peeled back to show the teeth?"

"I believe it."

On their way back to the car, Mr. Riddle stopped in a grocery store and bought two six-packs of canned dog food. He bought the cheapest kind available. Liz, who had once been "commercial coordinator" for the program, saw that they were largely cereals, not the variety that boasted of being all-meat. She asked him whether it made a difference; whether Girl needed more meat. Already, she felt proprietary, part of the odd "family" in the Pierce-Arrow. Don Derry's show would be more than willing to buy the performing dog beefsteak, she felt.

"Some meat, yes," the old man said. He sounded like a mother discussing her three-year-old's diet. "But the fact is dogs are also natural cereal eaters. Look at your wild coyotes and foxes. More than half their diet is grains, fruits, berries. Girl is no fussy eater. She's clean and neat and grateful, and she never begs. She understands the larder isn't always full. We've

22

seen our hungry days, when the carnivals weren't playing."

A half dozen black and Puerto Rican children had clustered around the locked car under the highway and were rapping at the windows. Alex growled and barked furiously, hurling his muscular yellow body against the frame of the car, raging at his tormentors. Girl slept in a furry heap in the dusty rear seat of the automobile.

Liz, a graduate of Mount Holyoke, raised in a proper home in a small Vermont town, still experienced vague fears of New York at night. There was something frightening, unpredictable about the children taunting the dogs. Beyond the car, where the cobbled street met the pilings sunken into the Hudson River, some men were washing automobiles. A hydrant had been opened. Water sloshed and sprayed across the area, soaking cars coming down the

125th Street exit, and forming icy filthy rivulets.

"If you youngsters will behave, and let me feed my dogs, you'll get yourself a free show," Mr. Riddle said.

The howling children looked at his snowy beard, at Mr. Riddle's pink face. They retreated from the Pierce-Arrow.

"Holy Jeez, he look like Sanna Claus," a tan boy said.

"Man, he sure do."

"Give us a present, man."

"Hey, Sanna Claus, them yoah dogs?"

"They certainly are, young fellow. Now stand back so's I let them out."

Liz shuddered slightly. She knew about street children. She glanced at the men washing cars. Some help there?

Alex, unloosing thunderous barks, leaped from the car, roared at the retreating children, then calmed down when Mr. Riddle, with an

24

old penknife, opened a can of dog food and set it before him on a sheet of newspaper. Girl yawned, roused herself, and walked stiffly out of the car. She moved, Liz saw, with venerable dignity.

"Girl always lets Alex eat first," Mr. Riddle explained. "Alex isn't too bright and we don't like for him to think he's being neglected. You know, as if he's the less favored member of the family."

Alex's flattened, black face buried itself in the gummy food. He bolted great chunks of food, snuffling, pawing, oblivious to the taunting children. The gang had run under the elevated highway. From behind a dusty metal pillar one of them shied a rock at Girl. It bounced off her flank.

"Now that isn't nice," Mr. Riddle said. "That isn't nice at all."

A soft-drink can flew from behind the pillar. Then a bottle. The missiles struck the cobblestones in front of Girl, ricocheted toward Liz. She pulled her leg away. A sense of isolation, of terror, filled her. She would have to move Mr. Riddle and his car and his dogs to a safer place. The program would be only too glad to put them up in a hotel.

Two of the children, one black, one beige, came out from behind the pillar. They held bottles in their hands. Mr. Riddle scratched his head and looked at them. He seemed full of pity, confusion—as if all his years on earth had taught him nothing about man's infinite capacity for cruelty.

"You boys stop that," Liz said. "Leave those dogs alone."

Alex, intent on his supper, ignored them. He raised his thick neck and square head, and kept swallowing in shuddering spasms.

"Watch me hit that ole dog in the head," one boy said.

"Yeah, we hit him the same time. Bombs away, man."

Mr. Riddle shook his head and walked toward them. "Now, children," he said. "Now children, I said I'd give you a free show if you behaved."

"Sanna Claus, you look out."

"Man, we bomb Sanna Claus."

"Girl," Mr. Riddle said. "Pick up that tin can and return it to the boy who tried to hit you with it."

The old dog's soft mouth embraced the can. She plodded toward the black boy and dropped the can at his feet.

"Hey," he said. "Hey, what that dog doin'?"

"Girl," Mr. Riddle said. "Which boys are holding bottles in their hands?"

Girl's tender brown eyes looked at the children. The others had come out from behind the column. She nudged the beige boy with her moist muzzle. Then put a soft, wet paw on the black boy.

"Hey, Hector, look at this crazy dog," the black boy said. "That dog doin' magic."

"Girl, which boy is wearing a blue shirt that says New York Mets on it?"

With no hesitation, Girl padded to a tiny boy with the face of an angel, and touched his shirt with her right paw. She looked at his hostile, dark face with a kind of tolerant acceptance of the human species, and for a swift magical moment, Liz saw an aura of light, a wonderful sweetness on the boy's face. It was a light that seemed to diffuse, to charge the cold dirty air, until all of the children were smiling, bending to pet Girl, speaking softly, captivated by the old dog.

"Normally we don't go along with these acts," Derry said. He had sitting around him,

in the familiar semicircle, a busty French actress, a country music singer in a suede suit
and gold boots, an elderly male character actor
who had written his autobiography, and a
black comedian. It had been a dull show. Lutz
Meminger, the orchestra leader, had had to
liven things up with fanfares and rim-shots.

"Animals?" the black comic asked. "Man,
I knew there was a gimmick when you ast me
on. Put the brothers on with the dogs. Want
me to sit up and beg?"

"Buddy, get the needle out," Derry said.
"I was saying animal acts are usually the same
old gimmick. We'll let the audience judge this
one."

"You let a animal on, you askin' for trouble," the comic babbled on. "Look how that
monkey take over 'Today.' They have to fire
him, he get so famous."

The male actor joined in: "It was like Gertrude Lawrence chasing Danny Kaye out of *Lady in the Dark*."

There was more show biz chatter while Mr. Riddle waited backstage with Girl at his side and with Liz holding his arm. He did not seem nervous.

"So welcome, Mr. Riddle, and the wonder dog, Girl!" Don Derry shouted. He got up and led the applause. Lutz Meminger's orchestra played "That Doggie in the Window." The audience laughed. The old man looked like a poorhouse Santa Claus out of uniform. The dog was obviously old, feeble, and friendly.

"Tell us about Girl, Mr. Riddle," Derry said.

"This here dog has a vocabulary of four thousand words. Taught her since she was a pup."

"I don't want to be rude, but my psychologist friends say that's impossible. A dozen

30

words, twenty words, okay. But four thousand?"

"That's correct, sir. This is no plain dog."

The director was taking audience reaction shots. People were smiling and nudging one another. They liked Mr. Riddle and Girl before they had done anything.

"Convince me," Derry said.

"Glad to. Girl, show us the drummer in that band. The man who plays the drums."

Girl's head looked about. She walked to the rear of the stage and placed a paw on the bass drum. Everyone applauded.

"*Fantastique*," the French actress said.

"Show us a man with a trombone," Riddle said.

The dog surveyed the band with loving eyes and found a trombone. This time she jumped up and put both paws in the musician's lap.

"A saxophone, Girl."

Girl turned her head. Without leaving the trombonist's lap, she leaned sideways and licked the saxophonist's black hand.

"Right on, Girl," the saxophonist laughed.

The applause was deafening.

"I have to say it's a good act," Derry said.

"It's no act, sir," Mr. Riddle insisted.

Girl picked out the bass fiddler, the flutist, and the man on vibraharp.

"That's no dog, that's a member of Local 802," Derry said. The audience did not laugh. "Mr. Riddle, can she double on clarinet and sax? Wear a size 37 suit?"

"I don't make no fake claims for Girl. She's just a dog, aged twelve, who learned a lot of words. Girl, there's a lady sitting in the third row and she is wearing a black dress with pearls, and has a nice head of red hair. You show her to me."

The woman to whom Mr. Riddle referred was Mrs. Fassnacht, the mother of the network's vice-president for programing. She adored Don Derry and never missed one of the shows. Girl padded down the stage. The cameras turned and found Mrs. Fassnacht. Gently, Girl put her head in the woman's lap. The dog did not drool, or rest heavily, or make a nuisance of herself. She rested her head a moment, withdrew it, and appeared to be smiling at Mrs. Fassnacht. The woman smiled back and patted Girl's head. Girl offered a cushionlike paw.

The applause was overwhelming. People were standing and cheering.

"Okay, okay," Derry said. "Now we'll find out how it's done. There's got to be a gimmick. There always is in these animal acts."

There were murmurings in the audience. In the wings, Liz Willis nudged Alan Groff. "Boss is making a mistake. People want to believe. They *believe* in that dog."

Groff grimaced. "Don is no dope. He's

figured out every magic act. He exposed that medium who claimed she heard voices."

"Alan, this is a smart dog," Liz said.

"Not only that, she's topping him."

Derry had gotten up. Amid much giggling from the other guests, he was inspecting Mr. Riddle's beard. "There's a whistle hidden in here," the star said. He raised the clouds of snowy hair so that the old man's face was covered.

"Nothing up his beard, nothing in his sleeves," Derry said.

"He needn't have looked. Right, Girl?"

Girl nodded. This time the audience gasped. There was something poignantly touching about the way in which Girl had agreed with her master.

"It isn't a whistle only a dog can hear?" Derry asked.

"No whistle."

"Your false teeth."

34

"No, sir. I mean, yes. I got a set of false teeth, but it don't mean a thing to Girl." Mr. Riddle clacked ivory choppers a few times.

"Take them out and give her orders," Derry said, triumphant. "It's his teeth. I heard them chattering. They're the signal he uses to move the dog one way and another."

"Hey, man," the black comedian said. "I didn't hear no clacking. You hear anything?" He turned to the other guests. They were on Mr. Riddle's side.

Derry appealed to the studio audience. "Who wants to see Girl take orders *without* Mr. Riddle's teeth?"

The applause was marginal. Mrs. Fassnacht, the network executive's mother, was *tsk-tsking*.

With a sigh, Mr. Riddle took out his teeth. His lower face collapsed. The beard looked like a batch of stained feathers.

"Give her an order," Derry commanded.

35

"Girl," Mr. Riddle said. "Shows the lady washin us yonder offastashe."

Girl trotted to the wings, took Liz Willis' plaid skirt in her tender mouth, and pulled her into view. The audience knew Liz. Derry often joked about her as the program's "Den Mother" or "Big Mama."

"It's Liz!" Mrs. Fassnacht shouted. She turned to her neighbors in the audience. "It's no trick. The dog is a genius."

"Girl, bring ush a mushical shoore Mr. Meminsha ushin."

Girl walked to the podium and looked at Lutz Meminger for his approval. Meminger secretly hated Derry. Derry had refused to pay for the new orchestrations. "Sure, Girl, you can have it," Meminger said. The dog put her mouth around the sheet music. Like a retriever bearing a mallard duck, she brought it to Mr. Riddle and dropped it at his feet.

"You're whistling silently," Derry said. "You're moving the dog somehow."

A teen-ager in the audience booed. A half dozen voices joined him. The French actress was explaining to the comic that the dog had supernatural powers, and that Derry could get in trouble if he insisted on challenging her.

When the show was in its final ten minutes, Derry stood Mr. Riddle behind a screen, with only his voice to direct Girl. The audience hooted again.

"It's no fake," a fat man called. "It's real."

"He proved it, Don, stop," Mrs. Fassnacht shouted.

From behind the screen, Mr. Riddle called out: "Girl, go to the sixth row and show me two Japanese gentlemen. One is in a gray suit, one is in a brown suit and both have cameras."

It took Girl eight seconds to walk down the aisle, raise her head and sniff out the Japanese tourists. The dog remained frozen between them, her tail waving in joyful arcs. The Japanese convulsed in laughter.

From behind the screen, Mr. Riddle's voice issued forth: "Girl, get back on stage and thank Mr. Don Derry for being so nice to us."

Girl returned and rested her shaggy head in the star's lap. The French actress was on her knees, hugging the mongrel. The audience rose and gave the dog and its master a thunderous ovation. It was the most sustained applause on "Don Derry Tonight" since the time Frank Sinatra and Senator Howard Baker appeared together in support of a Danny Thomas charity.

"Biggest mail pull in the seven-year history of the show," Alan Groff said to Liz Willis and young Ed Jackson, the writer.

"And the biggest phone response," Jackson said. It was four days after Girl and Mr. Riddle had made their TV debut.

"But Don won't allow an encore," Liz said. "He's full of excuses. Like we shouldn't have cheap acts. He wants us to book Begin and Sadat on split screen with himself as moderator."

Groff passed a hand over his pale face. "Has he seen the ratings? The audience surveys?"

"He's seen them," Liz said. "He says we've been building audience and the dog happened to hit us when we peaked."

"A five-point jump in the Nielsen?" Jackson asked. "Look how it happened. The first half hour, our usual rating. Then people must have started calling their friends. Spread effect. By the time he put the old man behind the screen, we were *doubled*."

Groff popped four Rolaids and drained a

glass of Saratoga Geyser water. "Liz, should we try? I think he's in the wet suit again."

The producer and the research girl confronted Derry in his office. He was in the diving suit, wielding a spear gun.

"The dog," Groff said. "People want her back."

"Don, she was beautiful," Liz added. "Not just a dog. A loving, intelligent creature. You should read some of the mail."

"Funny you should mention it," Derry said. "I've been doing a little investigation. Waiting a call from Professor Morcom of NYU. Expert on Animal Psychology. He's checking his schedule to see can't he come on with Riddle and expose him."

In a few minutes the professor called. Yes, he would be delighted. Yes, most of these trained animal acts were based on conditioning and reinforcing. Reward the dog, it performs.

"So you want Girl again?" Liz asked.

"And the old man."

Groff twisted his scrawny neck. "It may be tough. They're all after him. Carson, Griffin, 'Today.' Educational TV wants him to MC a show. Liz, can you deliver him?"

"Mr. Riddle is loyal to us," Liz said proudly. "He told me when I took him back to the Pierce-Arrow the other night, we'd always have first call on Girl, because we believed in him."

"*You* believed in him," Derry said.

Professor Morcom examined Girl for hidden microphones, buzzers, sensors, or other electronic equipment. She licked his hand. She rolled on her back, and raised her forepaws in surrender. Mr. Riddle sat on the last chair in the semicircle of singers, actors and other celebrities, and squinted through his steel-framed specs. Liz had bought him new suspenders and made him get his hair and beard washed and set. The snowy hair rose around his wrinkled face like a corona of absorbent cotton.

"All in order," Professor Morcom said. "I've looked Mr. Riddle over too. He's clean."

"Tell us how it's done," Derry said. "There's got to be a gimmick."

"Girl," Mr. Riddle said. "Which hand was that man poking you with?"

Girl licked the Professor's right hand.

"Girl, there was a lady in a black dress and pearls here last time. I don't know where she's sitting tonight, but you find her for me in the audience."

Morcom was shaking his head.

"Puzzled, Professor?" Derry asked.

The audience buzzed. People looked for Mrs. Fassnacht, the vice-president's mother.

"This is uncanny," Professor Morcom said. He tugged at his goatee and adjusted his bifocals. "You mean, the dog picked this woman out *four days ago*, and he's sending her to find her again, with no other instructions?"

"Prof, you're the expert on animals," Derry said.

It took Girl thirty-seven seconds to find Mrs. Fassnacht. Once again she placed her shaggy head in her lap. Mrs. Fassnacht kissed Girl's matted head.

"Girl, two rows back there's a young man in a black leather jacket."

Girl found him in as long as it took for her to walk the two rows.

"Show me the nearest Exit door, Girl," Mr. Riddle called.

The dog walked down the carpeted aisle and stopped at the door. The network pages applauded.

"I wish they'd both take it," Derry said. The audience did not laugh. "I mean, they're so smart they make me feel like I'm learning-disabled. A high-achieving dog. A goal-oriented dog."

"There's an empty seat in the fourth row from the back, Girl," Mr. Riddle said. "If Mr. Derry don't mind, please go sit there and be still till I call you. When I call your name, go to the young man in the blue uniform with gold braid, the one who just made goo-goo eyes at the young lady in the uniform."

The dog sniffed her way to the empty seat, crawled into it and sat down. She did not seem out of place as a member of the audience.

"Okay, Professor, how's it done?" Derry asked.

"I'm not sure."

"Signaling."

"If it is," Professor Morcom said, "it's the best signaling system I've ever seen. Even chimpanzees . . ."

Derry was silent. *Chimpanzees.* The one that had almost taken over the "Today" show.

Talking horses. Derry's parents had been in show business. On his deathbed, Derry's father had warned him never to compete with a child or an animal.

"Go ahead, Girl," Mr. Riddle called.

Girl slid from the seat and walked to the giggling pages. She sat between them, pawing the young man's blue trousers, then the girl's blue skirt.

"Animal conditioning is a relatively simple procedure," Professor Morcom said. "Chickens can be trained to walk a tightrope. Rabbits will play a piano. They do this for rewards. This dog is a bit more complex. There is a trusting relationship between master and dog. A kind of understanding."

"I'm not her master. Girl is my friend."

"That's right," Mrs. Fassnacht shouted from the audience. She led another round of applause.

"Girl, come back here and take a rest," Mr. Riddle said.

"How does he do it?" Derry persisted.

"I haven't the faintest idea," Professor Morcom said. "All I can tell you, Mr. Derry, is that Girl is a very smart dog."

The mail and phone response was even greater after Girl's second appearance. The program was inundated with requests from owners of brilliant parrots, genius armadillos, ponies who could do square roots. Derry sulked in his office. He was glad that the show was going off to Nassau. Undersea life, reefs, girls in bikinis. He was a big star. Often, the program went on the road because Derry was bored and needed sun, water, women. And he would be able to shelve the dog and the old man.

Fassnacht, the vice-president, called

Derry one afternoon and explained how the ratings had nearly doubled. Four dog-food companies wanted Girl to appear in their commercials. Two wanted exclusive contracts with her. Where had Mr. Riddle gone? Who could find him?

"Fass, I made this show," Derry said. "It's me, Don Derry, with my new style, my combo of entertainment and journalism, that created audience. I don't need a dog act."

"I'm afraid it's more than a dog act. My mother says it's like a spell that comes over the audience. People love that dog and that old guy. They're rooting for the mutt to get it right, to find the guy with the green tie, or the man with the saxophone."

"Fass baby, it's the same number every time. I can't let a dog dominate a major communications operation. This program is trendy, thinky, with-it. We deal in big ideas, big issues.

Show biz and news game, combined in one big lasagna. I mean, Fass, a *dog*?"

"That dog is important," Fassnacht said firmly. "I can't put my finger on it. Chemistry. Charisma. It fills a need. My mother says . . ."

When the vice-president dragged his mother in, Derry knew it was time to surrender —if only temporarily. "Okay, okay, Fass. Just once more, before we go to Nassau. For you and your mother, dig?"

"Wonderful, Don."

"I'll fix them," Derry said, after he had hung up. "I'll find a porpoise that'll make that mutt look retarded."

The star buzzed Liz Willis and ordered her to come in at once. "Book the old guy and the pooch for Friday," he said.

"Oh, marvelous, Don!"

"Why?"

"Well . . . the mail is tremendous. The

rating went way up again when we had Girl on."

"Everybody's in show biz," Derry said sourly. He sounded hurt, plaintive. Under the smooth plastic exterior, the boyish smile, the sharply tailored suits, Liz knew, was a worried, puzzled young man from a small town in Wyoming. Derry moved in perpetual fear that the vast sums of money he commanded, the enormous audiences, could vanish as easily as they had appeared.

"I know you aren't terribly enthusiastic about the dog," Liz said. "But people like her. They like the old man."

"They liked that chimp also."

"It didn't hurt the 'Today' show. It helped it succeed."

"Success like that I don't need. No, don't walk out on me, Liz. Look, I created this new concept in television journalism. Nobody thought to have this informal, loose way of doing big stories, major news. I taught those dumb news departments how to have fun with big issues. To reach people. It's important to me. A trained dog? Liz, baby, you read me?"

"Loud and clear."

Derry assembled his long reedlike figure and slithered out from behind the endless mahogany desk. He seized the script girl's wrist in a damp grip. "Liz, nobody appreciates me. I'm a force in America. I may run for the United States Senate. After I reform the media, I may become a university president. What are you doing for dinner?"

"I have a date."

"After the show."

"Sleeping."

"Ah. Alone? With a friend? Still dating Jackson? The serious newsman with the fast typewriter? Don't you know I buy and sell writers? I use up newsmen like Ed Jackson like they were paper clips. It's my concepts and my personality that have made this program."

"Please, Don. Let go." She shivered slightly. Derry was more to be pitied than hated. He had been making passes at her for several months. He had already warned her that if she kept seeing Jackson outside the office, the writer would be fired. But withal, Derry had something soft and pale and appealing at his core. What was it? Did he honestly conceive of himself as the man who had revolutionized television journalism with his breezy style? "I invented the byline piece, with the stand-up reporter," he once claimed. (The "Today" show had done it twenty years ago.) "Informal, casual journalism, it's mine," he boasted (ABC's local news had started it ten years ago). What appalled Liz was that not only did he make these claims publicly, he seemed to believe them. Worse, his breezy, gossipy, four-people-on-chairs technique rarely shed light on anything. The program, while amusing, usually consisted of a second-rate comic explaining the stock market (of which he knew nothing) or a fading actress promoting transactional analysis (of which she knew less). Instant experts, instant revelations, instant commentary. And none of it worth a page in any good book.

"That old bum," Derry said, after Liz had, like a schoolteacher, sent him back to his desk. He had tried to embrace her, resigned in defeat when she shoved him away. "What's his gimmick? What's his angle?"

"He has none."

"He has to. Everyone's got a hype, a net-net, a num-num."

"Mr. Riddle has none, Don. He likes animals, and he raised a smart dog."

Derry made a tent of his fingers and buried the lower part of his face in it. "I'm staying in town tonight. Meet me later for a drinkie. Flowers and soft music, Liz?"

"No, Don."

"Maybe the time is right for a lady producer. If Alan Groff keeps booking dogs, he may have to be replaced. You might be the new *Numero Uno*."

"Not that way, Don. But it's a kind thought."

The network's news department became interested in Girl and Mr. Riddle. The news director suggested taking Girl up to the animal behavior laboratories at New York University, where Professor Morcom ran rats through mazes, conditioned pigeons to press levers and get their rewards in corn, trained monkeys to work pinball machines. A film crew would go along and record Girl's meeting with the psychologists for the evening news.

Although the Don Derry show was not involved, the newsman asked if Liz would mind accompanying Girl and her aged master. Liz seemed to be the only contact with the old eccentric who lived in a battered car with two dogs.

After lights and cameras had been set up, Girl and Mr. Riddle were brought into a large, gymnasiumlike laboratory room, full of gauges, meters, testing apparatus, one-way glasses through which the psychologists could watch the animal perform.

"I suggest we test Girl's intelligence in simple problem solving," Professor Morcom said, "without Mr. Riddle present. Is that all right?" He looked at the old man.

"Heck, it's all right with me. Go on, Girl."

The thick tail wagged feebly. Girl had been sniffing at the caged white rats. She studied them with dark sympathetic eyes. The rats did not act afraid. They thrust their pink noses through the wire mesh, as if communicating in some vibrational way with the dog.

Girl was placed in a maze. She had to find her way out in a minute to beat the best time ever recorded by a white rat. Mr. Riddle, Liz, and the others watched from behind the one-way glass. On Professor Morcom's desk was a microphone through which they could talk to Girl.

"Now," Morcom said. "Let's see her find her way out."

They waited. The cameras rolled. Girl sat down in the middle of the walled labyrinth and whimpered twice.

"She isn't even trying," Morcom said.

"Course not," Mr. Riddle said. "Why should she? She's looking for me."

"There's a dog biscuit at the end of the maze," Morcom said plaintively.

"There's more to life than biscuits," Mr. Riddle said, almost angrily.

Girl sprawled in the maze. She seemed bored.

"You talk to her," the psychologist said to Mr. Riddle. He gave him the microphone.

"Girl, listen. They got you in some contraption with walls and funny turns and there's only one way out. You start walking, Girl, and find your way out, do you hear? There's a doggy biscuit at the end."

The old dog got to her feet. Her shaggy head was alert, her floppy ears perking. She wagged her tail, then galumphed through the tricky turns and corners of the maze in thirty seconds. She gobbled the biscuit.

"I guess she needs your voice," Morcom said. "That was a new record for the maze. Thirty seconds."

Later, with cues from Mr. Riddle, Girl set

a new record in working the monkeys' pinball machine. "Girl," Mr. Riddle said, "there's a machine there with a lever. Pull it with your mouth and see can you get the ball to jump around. You do it nicely, this man will give you another doggy biscuit."

As if tolerating the lunacies of humans, the dog plodded to the elaborate machine, put her mouth around the lever and worked the machine. She seemed to enjoy the game, trying to stop the bouncing rubber ball under the glass with her moplike paw, whimpering when the lights flashed.

"My goodness," the professor said. "She learned that in no time. The smartest rhesus monkey took an hour to master the technique."

"I told her what to do, and she understood," Mr. Riddle said.

Before they left, Girl beat a pigeon at Ping-pong, mastered the slot machines that spouted corn kernels, and found Professor Morcom's umbrella, which he had misplaced under a sink.

In his penthouse apartment on Fifth avenue, opposite the Metropolitan Museum, Don Derry watched the evening news, and saw the three-minute film on Girl's dazzling performance at New York University. After the dog had found the umbrella—on Mr. Riddle's orders—Morcom could only repeat what he had said on the Don Derry show. *A very smart dog. A unique dog. A loving dog.* But the how and why of its intelligence eluded him. It could not be measured, analyzed, put on a graph, turned into an equation.

Derry shuddered and turned the set off. An insecure man, one whose public geniality only underscored his hostile view of the world, the cutting edge in his personality, he wondered if he would come to be known as the TV star who was eclipsed by a dog. He would have to act if this continued, and act ruthlessly.

To publicize the week in the Bahamas, the cast of the Don Derry show appeared in costume. It was the Friday before they would fly to Nassau. The band wore junkanoo regalia. The guests were given flowery shirts. Derry wore his black wet suit, and demonstrated the aqualung, the underwater sleds, and the spear guns.

But the audience wanted Girl. When Mr. Riddle and the dog appeared, everyone rose. People cheered and whistled. Derry did not applaud. Behind the aquamask he was scowling.

"Girl," Mr. Riddle said, "some person on the stage is holding a weapon in his hands, a

59

kind of long spear he can kill fish with. Show us that weapon."

Unhesitatingly Girl walked toward Derry.

Derry cocked the weapon. It had a pistol grip and a trigger. He had used spear guns before. Once he had accidentally winged a seal when they were originating from the Seaquarium.

The audience gasped. Fassnacht, sitting with his mother, got to his feet. "What . . . ? What's he . . . ?" He could not believe it. Not their lovable Don, their superhappy host.

"*Ping*," Derry said out loud. "One squeeze, and right between the eyes."

There were boos and hoots from the audience. A man was shaking his fist.

"Only kidding, folks," Derry said. He aimed the gun at Girl's furry brow for a second, then raised it. "Only kidding."

"Go on, Girl," Mr. Riddle said. "Show us that gun for fish. It's only for fish."

Girl put a paw on the spear gun.

"Mr. Derry is right, folks," Mr. Riddle said. He stroked his beard. "He was only fooling. Wasn't he, Girl?"

The day after the Don Derry show arrived in Nassau, Derry and Alan Groff received telegrams signed by Roy Fassnacht and the network president. The star was sunning himself by the pool, reviewing the evening's guests. He would interview the head of the Department of Tourism, a troupe of Goombay singers, and the world's champion underwater divers, who would kill groupers for him.

Groff, Liz and the writers noticed that he was more relaxed in the sun. The change of scenery was good for him. The show would have to travel more, do more light features, use more humor. Derry was wrong to try to be an Alistair Cooke or an educational TV type.

The telegram upset him terribly.

KNOW YOU WILL UNDERSTAND THIS DECISION
BUT WE ARE BOOKING GIRL AND MISTER
RIDDLE AS REGULAR CAST MEMBERS TO AP-
PEAR NIGHTLY ON YOUR RETURN STOP RE-
ACTION YOUR ANGER WITH DOG APPARENT
TO MILLIONS VIEWERS AND MAIL IS DROWN-
ING US ONLY WAY MAKE UP IS TO HIRE DOG
AND KEEP AROUND AS SHOW MASCOT ETCET-
ERA BESIDES RATINGS ARE STILL POOR WE
FEEL SHOW NEEDS A COUNTERWEIGHT TO
YOU LIKE TREACHER WAS TO GRIFFIN OR
MACMAHON TO CARSON OR CHARLIE WEAVER
TO PAAR REALIZE THIS IS MAJOR STEP BUT
DOG AND RIDDLE SIGNED FOR THIRTEEN
WEEKS PLUS THIRTEEN REGARDS

"It's only for thirteen weeks," Groff said
placatingly. "The public will get tired of the
dog. Same act every night."

"Get my lawyers," Derry said. "Get my agents. They didn't consult me on this."

"We need that dog for a while, Donny. Roy Fassnacht is no gambler. He thinks Girl can save us. You know, we aren't the first talk show got into trouble because it got too heavy. Look at Frost, Cavett."

Derry's long jaw went rigid. "I'll be second banana to a flea-bitten dog," he said. "Me, a graduate of Wyoming State College."

Groff tried to appease him. He had girls sent to his room, one white, one black, one Chinese, all beautiful. Derry threw them out. The star went through the show listlessly that night. When they did the porpoise act, the audience kept shouting that they wanted Girl.

After the program, Derry found one of the writers and asked him about another dog feature they had done a year ago. A guest who trained special dogs. Where was he? Somewhere in Florida? The writer even remembered the guest's name.

63

At dawn Derry was on a chartered plane for Orlando, Florida. He hired a car at the Orlando airport, and after a few false starts, found a sagging frame house with a rusty cyclone fence around it. In the unkempt yard were abandoned auto parts—fenders, chassis, bumpers. On the chained gate was a sign:

STAY OUT

DANGEROUS DOGS

THIS MEANS YOU

J. B. HUGG

Derry looked for a bell, found none, then called Mr. Hugg's name a few times. A savage barking rose from the house. It was a fearful noise. At length a stumpy man with a pot belly came out of the house. He wore a vest over his naked torso. He stepped hesitantly down the broken porch steps. The man carried a Coke in one hand, a short whip in the other.

"Mr. Hugg? Mr. J. B. Hugg?" Derry remembered him. He had been slicked up for the TV appearance in a neat suit and a tie.

"Whut in hell you hootin and hollerin this early fer?" Mr. Hugg asked. "Had us a main last night, biggest of the year."

"It's me, Mr. Hugg. Don Derry from the television."

"Why it surely is. How yew, Mr. Derry?"

"Fine, fine. Look . . . can we go in? I have a private matter to discuss with you."

They sat in Hugg's kitchen and sipped coffee. Hugg offered Derry a glass of bourbon to go with the coffee, but the star refused. He was getting a migraine headache. The house reeked of dog turds.

"You know what it is to put out a contract?" Derry asked.

"Like the Mafia and all that. How they kill people."

"Right."

"You got troubles? Ah ain't the man to see. Got me enough troubles with the Humane Societies."

65

"I don't want to put out a contract on a person. I want to put out a contract on a dog."

"Dog?" Mr. Hugg poured a half tumbler of bourbon down his throat.

"Yes. Do you ever watch my program?"

"Cain't say as Ah do."

"That doesn't matter. This must be done in absolute secrecy. I want your best dog. Your champion of champions. He will be our hit man. That's another Mafia expression."

"Hit man. That's good. And whut do we all git for this?"

Derry gave him a crisp thousand-dollar bill. "This now. Your expenses come out of it, and you can keep the rest. When the contract is filled, I'll give you another two thousand dollars. You'd have to win an awful lot of fights to make that kind of money."

Mr. Hugg scratched his bald head. "They's a small problem. We don't use our fightin dogs to git after other animals. Can't

66

even use 'em as watch-dogs, 'cause they kill too good."

"This will be a favor for me. You and I will be the only ones who will ever know. I'll give you two thousand now. And three thousand more after the hit is made."

Mr. Hugg was mixing dry dog food with water in a metal pail. He laced it with cod-liver oil and ground fish heads.

"Reckon you got a deal. Two thousand now, three when we do the job." He scowled at the thick mush. "Don't seem right, somehow. Contracts, hit men. Sounds furrin."

Derry took from his coat pocket a map of Manhattan. Liz Willis had told him about the Pierce-Arrow parked under the West Side Highway. It was a car that could not be missed.

"Know what a Pierce-Arrow looks like?" the star asked Mr. Hugg.

"Ah surely do." Mr. Hugg tucked the bills

into his vest pocket. "Ah'll use me Wanda Sue. Ain't no dog in the world can fight that ole gal."

Three days later, while the Don Derry show was still in the Bahamas, Mr. Riddle decided the time had come to move on. He had made a nice few dollars with his appearances on television. Miss Willis and Mr. Groff had promised him more work, but he had the old urge again. He missed the county fairs, the volunteer fire department clambakes, the carnivals, where he could set up at the edge of the dusty grounds, put Girl through her paces, and pass the hat. That was real fun. Being close to people. Watching the children laugh and applaud.

Mr. Riddle was studying a road map on the hood of the Pierce-Arrow. He would head south. It didn't matter where. At the sign of the first fairgrounds, he would stop.

Girl and Alex were sniffing in mounds of garbage. Every now and then Girl would pick up an empty beer can or a cardboard box and shove it against Mr. Riddle's side. "Now, Girl," he would say, "stop that at once. Can't you see I'm concentrating? Please throw that junk in the river."

Fifty feet from the car the wintry Hudson River, iron gray and scummy, flowed to sea. Chunks of February ice gathered around the pilings. It was dusk of a damp New York day. Mr. Riddle had decided he would not wait for another call from the television people but would leave that night. He knew what Don Derry was thinking. Girl knew. Ever since the business with the spear gun.

A shiny green Oldsmobile pulled up and parked about ten yards from the Pierce-Arrow. It had Florida license plates. Mr. Riddle, intent on his map, paid no attention. Friendly Puerto Ricans often brought their cars below the highway to wash them. Some recognized Girl and fussed over her.

But the man who got out of the Oldsmobile was not a Puerto Rican. He was a fat, short white man with a bald head, wearing a checkered outdoor jacket and black trousers. He had a dog on a short leash.

It was a strange-looking dog, Mr. Riddle thought, long-headed, short-haired, with a twisty tail. It was dark-gray in color and it had small slanted eyes. "Why, I'll be dipped in molasses," Mr. Riddle said. "That there is a Staffordshire terrier. Ain't seen one since they outlawed the dogfighting in Tennessee. Used to have them Sundays. Terrible how them dogs went for each other's throats. Howdy."

Hugg did not respond. His eyes darted to the river bank, where amid mounds of snow and refuse, Girl and Alex gamboled. Hugg was

70

puzzled. Derry had mentioned only one dog, a gray-brown bitch about the size of an airedale. He had said nothing about a big yellow male, a sort of mastiff.

"The fighting ones is all bitches, isn't that right?" Mr. Riddle asked cheerfully. "Feller told me once that the females is deadlier than the male. That looks like a proper fighting terrier."

Mr. Hugg unhooked the leash from the Staffordshire terrier's collar. The collar was thick and studded. In professional mains, they did not wear them. Throats were favored targets. But this, Hugg reasoned, was a *hit*. There was no question about fairness or wagering. Derry explained it to him: contracts made no provision for giving an enemy a chance.

"Them's your dogs?" Hugg asked. The Staffordshire was quivering. Its snaky tail was pointing. It kept scratching its forepaws into the cobblestones. It made strangled noises, not of fear, but as if suppressing an emotional outburst.

"That's Alex and Girl. Alex is the big 'un. Mister, you better leash that terrier or we'll have us a dogfight on our hands."

Hugg hesitated. He had contracted to kill one dog. He had not the slightest doubt that Wanda Sue could kill both neatly and quickly. But it was a complication. Ganging up, if they were at all trained to attack, they might injure Wanda Sue, perhaps cripple her. She was worth over seven thousand dollars, an undefeated champion, a good breeder, a merciless killer.

Alex, his back bristling, pranced forward a dozen paces. He stood at attention, growling, yellow hairs rising in a ridge along his back. His blunt head was high and his eyes gleamed. Girl sat on her haunches, motionless. Her eyes never looked gentler. Her head drooped.

Hugg realized he would have to kill them

both. He patted the terrier's rump. "Attack," he said.

The terrier sprang forward. Alex charged. Hugg saw at once that the mastifflike dog, although brave, did not know how to fight. It came in with head too high, and did not use its paws for defense. The animals came together in a whirling, tumbling mass of legs, bodies, tails. Oddly, the terrier made no sound. It had stopped whimpering. It was intent only on Alex's throat.

"Stop 'em!" Mr. Riddle cried. "Dang you! Dang you, whoever you are! Police! Stop that! That's a fighting dog! Alex, run away! *Girl, come here!*"

It was too late. The dogs parted, slavering and shivering. Not a sound issued from Wanda Sue's throat.

Mr. Riddle, shaking, his beard fluttering, ran from his car toward the dogs. They were at each other again, teeth seeking throats, paws flailing, backs arching.

Hugg intercepted him and held him back by his suspenders. "Don't try it, mister. I seen your yaller dog start it. Let 'em fight it out."

Girl had gotten to her feet. She was sniffing the air, raising and lowering her head, making crooning sounds.

"It's over, anyhow," Hugg said. "Your mastiff shouldn't have come at Wanda Sue."

In a swift, lizardlike move, Wanda Sue lunged for Alex's throat, the soft skin beneath the jaw. She sunk her savage teeth deep into the dog's flesh, through hair, skin, muscle, deep into veins and arteries. Blood spurted from Alex's neck. He staggered backward and coughed, drowning in his own blood. Then he collapsed.

"You kilt him," Mr. Riddle shouted. "You done that a-purpose! Who in tarnation are you? What do you want with my dogs?"

"Attack," Mr. Hugg said.

Wanda Sue's broad snout and jowls were red with Alex's blood. She pawed the ground again and fixed her slanted eyes on Girl.

"Girl!" Mr. Riddle screamed. "Git away from that dog! Girl, come here!"

Mr. Hugg grabbed Mr. Riddle and held him against the side of the Pierce-Arrow.

Wanda Sue circled Girl warily. Her obscene head was close to the ground. The tail extended behind the hard body like a baton.

"Don't fight her, Girl!" Mr. Riddle bawled. "Please, Girl, talk to her!"

Girl was retreating. She moved creakily, clumsily. Wanda Sue crept on her belly. She was accustomed to dogs charging, fangs bared, paws flailing. The aged bitch was not her idea of an opponent.

Hugg ran from the car. Mr. Riddle wobbled after him.

Hugg brought the leash down on Wanda Sue's back. "Kill," he said.

Soundlessly the Staffordshire sprang at Girl. The old dog waited until the last fraction of a second, then rolled on her side, flattening her shaggy form against the cobblestones.

Wanda Sue, saliva streaming from her bloody mouth, her flat eyes astonished, sailed serenely over the prostrate dog into the frigid river. She struggled briefly in the scummy, cold water. Then the long head vanished in a swirl of gray ice. As she went under for the last time, she barked twice.

Hugg turned on Mr. Riddle. "That dog was worth seven thousand dollars. I got a mind to take it outen your hide." He raised the leash and advanced on Mr. Riddle. "Fact is, I am gonna take it outen your hide."

"Now, hold on, mister. You came here to kill my dogs. Fair is fair, and you got to take your medicine."

"That bitch of yourn put a spell on Wanda Sue. Ah seen dogs like that before. They put a conjer on other dogs."

"Girl never done no such thing. Girl understands, that's all."

Hugg was two steps away from Mr. Riddle's defiant figure—the old man was standing at attention, hands at the sides of his trousers—when they heard Girl. She was walking toward Hugg. Her lips were peeled back and Hugg could see the white, sharp teeth and the crimson gums. He knew dogs. He knew when they could kill.

"Call that bitch off," Hugg said. "What is she doin'?"

"You got her riled."

A low, deep growl, something more than ordinary canine menace, issued from Girl's mouth. Hugg's raised arm froze. Girl was crouching, her legs tensed, her eyes no longer gentle.

"Now look what you done," Mr. Riddle said. "Girl, it's all right, you don't need to get so mad. Please, Girl, listen to me. It's all over."

When the Don Derry show returned from the islands, Liz Willis had difficulty locating Mr. Riddle. The network brass, unhappy with the ratings, wanted a big publicity campaign about signing Girl, the Wonder Dog.

Derry, getting fitted for a ski suit and custom-made ski boots—he had decided to move the show to Aspen for a week so he could learn to ski—smiled to himself Liz would never find the old man and the mutt. His friend in Florida would see to that.

Fassnacht, the network president, Groff, and several sales executives sat in Derry's office, pleading with him to take the dog on as a regular. Three times a week? Two? They were drowning in mail. It wasn't just the dog's

78

intelligence, her mastery of language, or whatever system it was Riddle used to make her perform. People liked Girl. She was kind, patient, tolerant. The public craved gentleness. A relief from all the violence on TV.

"Okay, okay," Derry said. "I'll be generous. Twice a week, for a ten minute spot. The writers will have to think up gimmicks. Listen to Donny. People will get bored. It's a good act, but it's only an act." He could be magnanimous. But why hadn't Hugg called? Why had he not come for his three thousand dollars?

There was a knock at the door. Liz Willis entered. "I found them," she asked.

"*Them?*" Derry asked.

"Mr. Riddle and Girl. They were having the car fixed to go south. The mechanic at the garage called us. He wanted to see Girl on the show again."

"Hooray!" Fassnacht said. "Donny, we got us a deal!"

Mr. Riddle and his dog walked in. Everyone except Derry cheered.

"Nice Girl, nice poochie," Groff said. He got up and began to tickle Girl behind the ears, the way she had always liked it. But the dog ducked her head and slunk away.

"You know we want you on the show regularly," Fassnacht said.

"Thank you kindly, sir," Mr. Riddle said. "But Girl and me are moving on."

"This is important to us," the network president said. "We'll make it worth your while. All the dog biscuits she can eat."

"Things have changed," Mr. Riddle's eyes sought the ceiling. "Someone tried to kill Girl. Yes, it's true."

"That's dreadful!" Liz cried.

"Why?" Groff shouted. "Who would dare—?"

"I have my ideas." The old man patted Girl's head. "Girl, there's a man in this room tried to have you killed by a bad dog. Show us that man."

"This is insane," Derry said.

Girl crouched, head resting on the carpet. Her dark red lips curled. The bared teeth, the upturned snout spoke of the ancient law of club and fang, a jungle response. Growling ominously, Girl crept toward Derry's ski boots. Then she stopped and placed a paw on the boot. Her eyes were burning.

"This is ridiculous," Derry croaked. "A mutt accusing me. Alan, get them out. Liz, get rid of them."

Girl kept her paw on the boot. The low rumbling from her throat did not cease.

"She won't hurt you, Mr. Derry," Mr. Riddle said. He sounded full of an old man's regrets. "She would never hurt nobody. You see, that was part of her intelligence. She had no meanness. Until, until . . ." He began to weep, then took off his spectacles and wiped them on his flannel sleeve. Tears streamed down his cheeks and soaked his beard. Liz came to him and put an arm around his shoulder.

"Mr. Riddle, don't cry, please. We all love Girl. Everyone who saw her loved her."

"It don't matter no more. I'll try to train her again, but she's an old dog."

"What the hell is this? Who tried to kill her?" Fassnacht was on his feet, staring at the growling dog. Every time Derry pulled his booted foot back, the dog would advance, keeping one paw on the laces.

"Who the hell knows?" Derry shouted. "He's crazy. They're both crazy."

Mr. Riddle replaced the glasses on his nose. "I can forgive you trying to kill Girl. But I'll never forgive you for what you made her become. That dog never growled at no one, never threatened no one in her life. Now look. Now look what she's become. Come on, Girl."

Girl unloosed three murderous barks at

Derry, removed her paw, and followed Mr. Riddle out of the office.

"You book crazies, you see what happens?" Derry asked. He was trembling. "That's the end of animals on this program. Lousy, vicious mutt."

A few days later, J. B. Hugg sent in a bill for ten thousand dollars—three thousand for the balance of his fee, which seemed odd to Derry since he had failed to fulfill the contract, and seven thousand for his prize bitch, Wanda Sue, whom, he claimed, had been shot by Mr. Riddle. There was a veiled threat in the letter that unless Derry came across, Hugg would tell the newspapers. Derry immediately wrote a check, then called his tax accountant, to see if it could be claimed as a deduction. The tax man did not understand the TV star, who kept babbling about "putting out a contract on a dog" and about another dog who was a "hit man." He decided Derry needed psychiatric care.

In three months' time, Derry's ratings were so low—he kept insisting on more "thinky" features: stock market analyses, geriatrics, obesity, the Common Market—that the network started alternating his show with old horror films. Fassnacht predicted that his contract would be terminated in another thirteen weeks.

Some months later, Liz Willis took a trip to Macon, Georgia, with her fiancé, Edward Jackson. They went so that Liz could meet Jackson's parents. Both young people had left the Don Derry show. Liz was now an assistant director on a daytime quiz program. Jackson was writing newscasts. The Derry show was in its terminal weeks.

Leaving Macon after a three-day visit, Liz noticed a ferris wheel and an encampment of gaily painted vans and booths. A sign, flapping in the summer breeze, proclaimed the Annual Volunteer Fire Department Carnival and Barbecue. As they slowed down for the traffic around the fair grounds, Liz thought she saw a familiar figure.

"Ed, stop a minute. I see him. I *think* I see him."

"Who?"

"Mr. Riddle."

They parked underneath a grove of pin oaks. At one side of the admission booth they saw the old man. It was unquestionably Mr. Riddle. But whereas once he had been sprightly and upright, a vigorous old fellow, he now looked bent and shriveled. A dozen people—mostly children—had gathered around him. There was a dabble of applause, some laughter.

Hopping in the red dust was Mr. Riddle's new dog.

"Little Girl," Mr. Riddle was saying, "where is the lady in the blue dress who is carrying a big blue bag? Little Girl, that is *wrong*. You try again, please."

A smallish gray-brown mongrel, half the size of Girl, bounced, tail wagging, through the crowd, then rested a paw on the blue sneaker of an elderly lady. It looked at Mr. Riddle for approval.

"Cute as a button," the woman said.

"And smart as paint," a man said.

"Little Girl, show me the boy with the balloon. He's a redheaded boy."

The dog—she was much friskier than Girl —turned her shaggy head, looked at the children, hesitated, then leaped playfully on a boy holding a balloon.

"That's pretty good, Little Girl. Folks, this dog understands me. No magic, no tricks. But we have to eat also, so I'll pass the hat, if you don't mind."

Mr. Riddle shuffled through the small crowd, collecting dimes and quarters. He bobbed his snowy head in gratitude. A terrible sorrow drenched Liz. She squeezed her fiancé's hand. "Oh, Ed. It's so sad. Should we talk to him?"

"Why not? He always liked you."

Jackson dropped a dollar in Mr. Riddle's battered brown hat. The old eyes looked up. He seemed exhausted.

"Say, I recollect you. The young man who wore that yellow sweater all the way up to his neck." He saw Liz's smiling face. "And Miss Willis. Say, what a nice surprise."

She embraced him. Little Girl jumped on her slacks, pressing two paws against her thigh.

"Little Girl, you cut that out," Mr. Riddle said.

"Is she related?"

"To Girl? I'm afraid not."

"And Girl?" Liz asked.

"Oh, she died. As we all have to, dogs included." With a palsied, liver-spotted hand, he transferred the coins from the hat to his pocket, then jammed the hat on his mop of white hair.

"Wasn't the same after that business in New York," Mr. Riddle said. "No fault of you folks. But that fellow Derry. He misunderstood us, I guess. Girl was never the same. Did what I asked like always. But . . ."

"She wasn't as gentle, I guess," Jackson said helpfully. "What did happen, Mr. Riddle? Who tried to kill her? Why did she try to attack Don Derry?"

"It don't matter no more. It's past. It was just that the love went out of her. She liked me, all right, and she obeyed me, but the love was gone. The love she had for other people. When she put her paw or her snout on someone, it wasn't just a trick. Girl was saying something. Whole lot of things."

Liz got to one knee and tickled the young dog's ears. Little Girl rolled on her back, four feet up, surrendering her floppy body. "This new one is adorable, Mr. Riddle. Are you sure she isn't related to Girl?"

"No, Girl had no issue. I found this pup in the street in Memphis. She reminded me of Girl so I took her. She won't never be as smart as Girl. No dog could. Fact is, she's sort of mischievous. But we'll manage." His eyes brightened and he tipped his hat gallantly to them. "We'll move on, if you don't mind. Got to work the other side of the grounds."

Liz hugged him again. She kissed his coarse red cheek. He fidgeted, waved to them, and shambled off.

The two young people heard his cracked voice once more as they walked toward the car.

"Little Girl, show me the baby carriage. Not that one, Little Girl, the one that's got a parasol tied to it, and a lady in a yellow dress pushing it . . ."

And the laughter. The delighted voices of children.

"Don't cry, Liz," Jackson said. He held the automobile door open for her. She pressed a handkerchief to her face.

They drove off. Liz turned around once. The clouds of red dust, the tinkly calliope music, the rotating ferris wheel, the joyful shouts and lingering cries seemed to her the essence of a thousand summers, a thousand happy places, thousands of good times. And in the midst of them, in the heat of the lazy day, among the garish booths and creaky rides and cotton candy and frozen custard, the old man, it seemed to Liz, would wander forever with his gentle, intelligent dog, finding the man in the polka dot shirt, the lady in the orange dress.

S